LEGS
A short story

By

Travis Heermann

Bear Paw Publishing
Lakewood, Colorado

www.travisheermann.com

Sometimes Andy wished Joe would just shut the hell up. Joe raised his arms like someone had just scored a touchdown. "Hey, baby! Gimme some sugar!"

Jackie shut the car door and lifted her sunglasses.

Andy tossed down the hammer he'd been using to drive in tent stakes and used the picnic table to lever himself upright.

Jackie rolled her eyes at Joe's outburst—perhaps her smile had even faltered for the briefest moment—but still she came down toward the half-erected tent. Andy couldn't take his eyes off her. Smooth, tan legs disappeared into tasteful white shorts, and her gray NYU tank-top fit her like a sheer nylon. A sigh inflated behind Andy's breastbone like a helium balloon, a sigh he had to hold back.

Joe waited for her to get close enough, then threw his arms around her and squeezed her like a bear, laying a kiss across her lips. "How's the most amazing woman I know?"

She smiled up at him from chest level. "Fabulous."

As Joe released her, she gave Andy a stunning smile and wiped her lips. "Hey, Andy."

He swallowed hard and looked away, thrusting his hands into his pockets. "Hey."

Andy sensed she would have given him a hug, too, but Joe pulled her close and kissed her again. She only resisted a little. Or was Andy only seeing what he wanted to see?

Dammit.

The one beer in his belly turned leaden, and he headed

for the outhouse fifty yards up the path, looking away, looking at everything, looking at nothing, and wishing that sigh would go away. As he walked, the aluminum-and-plastic legs filled the bottom half of his blue jeans with bulges that weren't quite right, moved in ways that weren't quite natural. He rubbed the joint where one of the soft foam rubber cups fit over the end of his femur.

"Hey, Andy," said another woman's voice, stopping him in mid-flight.

She stepped out of the passenger seat of Jackie's powder-blue Prius.

He stopped and his legs wobbled. "Oh, hi, Christine." Great. Now he would have to spend the weekend with Christine's beady eyeballs attached to him. Just great. A pasty muffin-top of flesh hung between her blue jeans and tank top. "You got a haircut."

"Yeah, yesterday." She ran her fingers through thin, mousy brown strands, biting her lip. "You like it?"

He shrugged. "Sure."

"How's school?"

"I'm taking a couple of semesters off."

"Oh. I didn't know that."

Jackie said to Joe, "So this is what you call 'Camp-O-Rama?'"

"Baby," Joe said, "we're just getting warmed up. Beer is on ice, ribs are ready for barbeque, and the boat is raring to go."

Jackie nodded with appreciation. "It has promise. Hey, Chris, isn't the lake gorgeous?"

"May I offer you a beer, madames?" Joe said with mock

formality. "This vintage is a particularly good hour..."

Andy headed for the toilet again. Why had he let Joe talk him into this? The sigh finally escaped. At least with Christine here, he might have some distraction, rather than having to listen to Jackie swap bodily fluids with Joe for three days and wishing every single moment that it was with him instead.

Their campsite of several dozen square yards was carved from the Adirondack forest of oaks, birch, and alders, adjoining the sandy shore of Sacandaga Lake. To keep his mind occupied, Andy busied himself with putting up the tent.

Joe slapped some dirt off his hands. "So you women-folk set up the kitchen and home base while Andy and I put the boat in the water."

Jackie put her hands on her hips. "Did you seriously just say that? What century are you from? You want me barefoot and pregnant, too?"

Joe replied with a smirk, "Don't get ahead of yourself." He turned to Andy. "Let's go, buddy."

Andy followed him, just like he always did.

Andy had known Jackie was special from the first moment he saw her, six months before. He and Joe had been sitting in their favorite bar in Glens Falls, a place with cheap beer but still frequented by high-quality women their age, when he saw her walk in with a group of attractive friends. All of them were dressed to kill.

"Holy shit, Joe, look."

Joe whistled softly.

Even in such a group, she shone like a beacon. Andy's heart jumped up into his throat. Joe was having the same reaction.

Andy said, "I'd give anything for a woman like that."

Joe's attention was fixed on her like a laser. He slid off his stool. "I'm gonna talk to her."

Andy rolled his eyes. "Here he goes again."

Joe crossed the room and initiated a conversation with the girls, making it look like the easiest thing in the world. A slice of envy went through Andy, just like it always did at times like this. Joe had the looks and natural charisma that allowed him simply to walk into those situations without fear, an ability that Andy could only dream of having. Plus, Joe had legs.

Andy sipped his beer and rubbed the half-numb itchiness inside the cup at the end of his right thigh. Joe schmoozed the ladies. Andy couldn't hear over the music, but when she looked at Joe, her eyes sparkled.

A minute later, Joe returned to the table. "We're in."

Ten minutes later, Andy and Joe were neck deep in babes. Being Joe's friend had its benefits. Twenty minutes after that, Joe and Jackie couldn't take their eyes off each other, and Andy was mostly left out of the conversation with the other three women.

One of them—her name was Marie—sensed Andy's discomfort and turned to him to make polite conversation. "So you guys are good friends?"

"Yeah, since junior high."

Joe chimed in, "Buds for life." He stuck out a fist.

Andy grinned at him and knuckle-bumped.

"I have to say, you're an unlikely pair."

Joe said, "Hey, what do you mean by that?"

"You two are just so ... incongruous."

"Huh?"

Andy said, "She means we don't match up very well."

"Oh. Well, see, Andy here has artificial legs and—"

The women said various things at this discovery, as people always did, things like "Oh, I hadn't noticed," or "I'm sorry," or "That's terrible."

Andy said, "I manage." No need to call their attention further to his freak-ness.

Joe said, "So back in junior high he didn't take well to names like 'Stumpy' or 'Stubby.' I took care of that for him."

Andy said, "And Joe, on the other hand, didn't deal well with words like 'equation,' 'theorem,' and 'preposition.'"

Joe said, "True." He held up his beer glass to Andy. "To stumpy equations."

Andy clinked with him. "May they only use plus and minus signs."

Jackie smiled at him and nodded, raising her glass, too. Andy's heart took off like a herd of mustangs. She was in law school at NYU. Joe had a football scholarship to Syracuse, but couldn't keep up his G.P.A. without Andy's help. Joe's parents had money, but that wasn't enough to keep him in school. Andy had an academic scholarship to study computers at State University, but without Joe as the linchpin of his social life, he had lost interest and had to take a break.

An hour later, Jackie and Joe were dancing alone to the jukebox, the other women had gone off to another bar, and Andy sat alone, again, watching their legs slide and brush to the music.

Joe rested a wrist over the steering wheel of the black Dodge Ram, dappled with moving spots of sunlight through the trees. "Hey, man. You oughta know that Chris likes you. That's why she came along."

Like Andy and Joe, Christine and Jackie had been friends since grade school, neighbors. A familiar weight settled back in Andy's chest. "Really?" As if he didn't already know.

"Oh, come on, man. Show some enthusiasm. Here's a chance to get some. I've done worse."

"And regretted it." Andy snorted. "'Get some.'"

"Don't give me that romantic bullshit. Sometimes you just need to get laid. I got rubbers. Here." He held out his fist across the seat.

Andy opened his palm and Joe dumped two square packets into it. "She's not my type."

Joe rolled his eyes. "When was the last time you got laid, buddy?"

Never.

Joe nodded at the silence. "Exactly. For Christ's sake, that's what camping is for! That and beer."

"Thanks, O Great Lord of the Camp-O-Rama."

"Let me tell you something. If there's a woman you want, you got to go for it. You know what I mean?"

"Not exactly."

"Look, man, we've been friends for years. I've watched you for years. I'm going to be honest here, 'cause you need it. You sit back and pout at parties, bars, whatever, and act like the universe owes you pussy, like if you just sit there long enough, a woman is going to come to you, fall out of the trees or something. Like you need an amazing woman to discover you or something, to get you."

Andy's face heated.

"Let me tell you. It never works that way. Fucking never. A woman likes a man with balls enough to go after her, to at least make a move."

Andy pursed his lips.

"You still have a dick don't you? So quit polishing it yourself. If there's a woman you want, buddy, go after her, for Christ's sake. But in the meantime, there's a girl over there who obviously digs you. It won't take much. And get this." Joe elbowed him. "Jackie says Chris is a virgin. Christ, man, I've never had sex with a virgin!"

"Okay, okay, fine. I'll think about it."

"That's the spirit! As for the legs thing, think of it as a positive. Like maybe you're just the right height to eat pussy standing up."

"Douche bag."

Joe laughed. "So put the hot dog in the bun." Joe elbowed him again. "Have her cuddle the cannelloni." Another elbow. "Mount her like a deer."

Andy couldn't help cracking a grin.

Joe chuckled. "Polish the rocket. Hide the salami."

Andy put the condoms in his pocket. "Take the log to the beaver."

"Take One-Eye to the uh ... orthodontist."

"Optometrist, dumbass."

"Whatever."

They laughed.

Andy throttled up the boat and pointed it toward the distant cove amidst the tree-swathed mountainsides. The wind and spray of water on his face drew out a smile in spite of his mood. The power of the Cobalt 222's 320-horsepower engine surged through the craft, and he gripped the controls tighter.

As the water slid by under him, out here in the middle of the lake, the power of the engine vibrated up through his prostheses. He imagined what it might be like to dance on his own feet, not stumble around in a grotesque parody of natural movement. Bitterness rose on the back of his tongue again. A few tons of screaming metal and glass had ended his dancing career back in junior high.

He aimed the boat toward their campsite. As the small promontory emerged from the tree-swathed distance, a figure appeared on the shore. His stomach flipped over and his mouth went dry. Jackie had already changed into her bikini and was arranging the coolers for pickup. He throttled back and eased the boat in. Jackie leaned over to set down a cooler. She had an ass that was sent from God.

Christine came down through the trees, wearing a shapeless black one-piece with a yellow sarong wrapping her pale legs. She flapped a hand at him.

When Joe returned, they took off across the lake. At the helm, Andy felt his spirit rise with every lift of the bow. Christine sat alone in the bow, while Jackie and Joe sat behind him, laughing into the wind. Joe and Jackie made the waterskis look like child's play. Even Christine, looking nervous and uncertain, managed to get up out of the water after three tries. When she smiled, she wasn't terrible looking.

Jackie slid up beside Andy while Joe kept an eye on Christine trailing behind. "I saw this thing about a guy with prosthetic legs who got to be a champion waterskier."

"Oh, yeah?"

"Want to try it? It's not impossible you know."

"I'm driving the boat."

She met his gaze. "Joe can drive the boat."

He pretended to check their speed.

She sighed a little. "So, you like her?" Her gaze poked him again, so sparkling with intelligence.

He shrugged.

"She's really smart. Nice, too."

He wanted to say, *Not as smart as you.*

"So you're going to try skiing?"

Her eyes dragged a tingle up his spine. It suddenly seemed as if it meant a great deal to her for him to try. "I'll think about it. Maybe tomorrow." Maybe he actually would.

"Hey, baby," Joe called. "Grab me a brew."

She rolled her eyes, then turned away to reach for the cooler.

Andy's gaze flicked toward her glistening legs, the dew drops of sweat and tanning oil gathering on micro-fine down, traveling up to the little nest just under her buttocks as she bent over the cooler—

Stop it! She's your fucking best friend's girlfriend. It wasn't that Joe didn't deserve her but ... well, yeah it kind of was that. Joe had been with dozens of women. Why did he have to have this one? Then again, what the fuck would a woman like her want with half a man?

The yipping howls of coyotes echoed from the distant shore of the lake. "Cool," Andy said.

"Hmm?" Christine said.

"The coyotes are cool."

"Cool, but a little creepy, too. It almost sounds like they have a language."

Andy settled back against a log with the last beer from one cooler, enjoying the warmth and fuzziness of the campfire. But he had to be careful that the heat didn't melt his legs. Even these cheap models cost more than some people's homes.

The drinking games had abated momentarily. Joe and Jackie's lips slid around and around each other's at intervals. Andy's swimming head almost let him ignore it.

Christine sidled up next to him. "Does it hurt?" She laid a hand on the denim concealing the knobby rubber and aluminum where a knee should have been.

He shifted. "It's okay now."

"What about back then? Jackie says you were thirteen."

He nodded, took a deep breath and let it out. He could remember what it was like to grow and play and run. But he had never danced.

"I'm sorry." Her hand slid up, tentatively, trembling. He smelled the beer on her breath.

His ears grew hot. "Car accident. I don't remember it anymore, though."

She covered her mouth with both hands. "Oh, my God, that's awful!"

Andy shrugged again. He didn't want pity. He got enough of that from himself. "Sometimes it's like I can still feel them, like someone is tickling my foot, or my knee aches. They call it phantom sensation."

"Maybe part of your brain remembers."

"Maybe." But he wished it would forget.

Her hand went back to his leg, and her fingers passed the edge of the foam cup, warmed the flesh of his thigh. He looked at her hand as if from a distance, then at Joe and Jackie making out a few feet away. He wondered, *Should I be feeling something for this girl now?* He held his beer with both hands.

"Would you show me?"

The pleasant fuzziness in his mind smeared clean. Jackie giggled and whispered in Joe's ear. Andy had to get out of here. "I gotta go piss." He stood up, wobbling slightly.

Christine sighed.

He usually avoided getting drunk. Inebriation complicated ambulation, and navigating uneven ground in the dark made things even dicier. As he walked off into the woods, the darkness of leafy shadows closed around him, and his shoulders snapped tighter. The black truck and trailer loomed beside him, a hulking steel shadow between him and bushes.

God, what would he do to have a woman like Jackie? Anything.

Footsteps echoed in the distance, and a beam of silver-blue light flicked through the trees, coming nearer. The footsteps approached down the asphalt path, the light bobbing in time with the steps, maybe from a height of six feet. Was this person wearing a light on a hat? Long seconds passed, and Andy's beer-fuzzed ears detected a strange quality to the footsteps. The dancing beam drew near, passed along the side of the pickup truck.

The sound of the footsteps.

Not footsteps at all.

A tall shapeless figure passed by the front fender of the pickup. The beam resolved into two separate beams, set close together like eyes, and turned onto Andy's face. He raised a hand and shielded his eyes, squinting and blinking against the glare. Five heartbeats. Ten.

Then the beams turned away, and the footsteps resumed.

But the footsteps were wrong. Human feet did not sound like clop clop clop. Andy's throat clenched again and his belly went cold.

He blinked to try to clear his vision. When it finally did, the beam and figure had wavered off into the night. It was as if a great fist had suddenly released him. He bolted back toward the firelight, cold gripping the back of his neck. He stumbled over a tree root and sprawled face-first over the log, crashing into Christine. The rough log gouged into his torso and his prosthetic legs flailed.

Christine covered her mouth again, eyes wide. "Oh, my God! Are you okay?"

Expletives spewed out of him. His face burned, and his belly ground across the log.

"Buddy! Look out!"

Jackie's eyes were big and blue, brimming with concern.

She reached for him. "Are you okay?"

"Fuck! No, I'm not okay!" He lurched his dead aluminum and plastic weights around, gathered them, and slung himself to his feet again.

Christine raised a hand to help him, touched him, but he threw it off.

"I'm a fucking idiot retarded fucking cripple who's afraid of his own shadow!" He continued to swear as he stormed off into the night, clenching his jaw against all the pain.

He looked out across the moon-dappled lake. Loons called in the distance. The shore-side boulder grew hard under his ass, but he wasn't ready to go back and apologize for his outburst. He wasn't an outburst kind of guy, and his guts churned.

Footsteps approached.

He wished it was Jackie.

"Exquisite evening, eh?" said an unfamiliar voice.

Andy jumped and spun.

"Sorry to scare you," the man said, his voice deep and sonorous, a little rough, like a combination James Earl Jones and Russell Crowe.

"You didn't." Andy sat on his trembling hands.

"I'm camped a few slots down the line. Thought I'd go for a pleasant walk."

Andy grunted.

The man wore flip flops, khaki beach shorts, and a white, gauzy shirt that glowed in the moonlight, unbuttoned to a reveal a washboard torso. "Call me Moe Dee." He extended a hand.

Andy shook it, and it was smooth and firm, warm. "Andy."

"A pleasure, Andy. Mind if I join you? My friends were supposed to arrive this evening, but they were detained until tomorrow. I'm alone and bored witless."

Andy gestured at a nearby boulder.

Moe Dee sat, and lithe, toned legs stretched out before him. He was taller than Joe. "Those your friends back there?"

Andy nodded.

"So what are you doing out here? One of those girls back there looked like she had your name on her."

Andy sighed. "Just needed some time alone."

"Am I disturbing you?"

"Nah. Feel free."

"I do, most of the time."

"What?"

"Feel free."

Andy kicked the heel of his sneaker into the moist earth. "Must be nice."

"It's the only way to live. Spend enough time in prison and you swear to never go back."

Andy edged away. "You been in prison?"

"I was speaking figuratively. People put themselves in prisons of their own making. But you might say I spent a long time in a prison of sorts."

"You don't look that old."

"I'm older than I look."

"What kind of name is Moe Dee? Sounds like a rapper."

"Nickname. Long story." Moe Dee leaned back and stretched his long, lithe legs. "So what kind of prison do you live in, Andy?"

Andy's legs twitched. One knee joint squeaked. He needed to oil it.

"Prosthetic leg?"

"Two."

"Looks like you manage."

"I manage."

Moe Dee's voice slowed and deepened. "But it is the bane of your entire existence."

The weight on Andy's chest returned, heavier than ever, with a strange fuzziness rippling across his scalp.

Moe Dee's voice grew quieter, and Andy had to listen closely to hear. "You wish everyday to have been allowed to be a whole man, to stand to your full height on your own flesh, to walk with surety and confidence, like your friend back there."

Andy swallowed hard. The words rang in his ears, drilled into his mind.

"To have your girlfriend love you more."

"I don't have a girlfriend. That's just a girl."

Moe Dee's gaze glittered. "There's somebody else you want."

Andy stood and turned away.

"Somebody you love."

"Fuck, man! You're a stranger and we're sitting out here in the dark and you can tell that?" How then could Joe not see it? How could Jackie not know? "What are you doing, spying on us?"

"I saw you all from the road. Observing people is one of my talents. And I'm not judging you, Andy. That's the absolute last thing I would do. But I might be able to help you."

"How about you show me how to turn it off?"

"How about I show you how to turn it on? In her."

"Like what, give me some good lines I can use on her to make her break up with my best friend and fall madly in love with me?"

"Have a seat. Let's talk."

Andy sat.

"My friends were coming up to do some serious partying tonight. Serious."

"You mean like weed or drugs or something?"

"No, better."

Andy couldn't remember the last time he'd looked at a man and thought, *What a good-looking guy.* Such a though had never once crossed his mind. A twinge of homosexual panic shot through him. "You mean like swingers or something?"

Moe Dee smiled. "Indeed. But we have some ... chemical enhancements as well."

"Really? Sounds wild." The kind of stuff he had only read about in Penthouse. "Like Ecstasy or something?"

"No, better. Totally new. It's called 'H'."

"Heroin?"

"I said 'new.'" Moe Dee put a hand in his pocket and withdrew a handful of capsules that glowed like pearls in the moonlight. "Just one of these and the most frigid woman on earth will surrender to the most intense passion she has ever experienced. Trust me, you want to be nearby when this happens. She will love every second of it and experience no morning-after remorse, and neither will you. Afterward, it will all feel like the most natural thing you have ever done. And it's like Viagra on crank. Sodom in a bottle. Just give one of these to everybody, including yourself, and we'll have us a grand time."

"Wow."

"Wow, indeed."

Andy found himself reaching out, but Moe Dee put them back in his pocket. What the fuck was he doing? This guy was some kind of drug dealer. He stood up. "I should go back."

Moe Dee's eyes glittered again, and his voice rumbled up Andy's spine. "You should. But one last question. What would break you out of your personal prison, Andy?"

Andy rubbed his hands. "My dad always said you can wish with one hand and shit in the other, and see which one gets filled first."

"Indulge me. I'm not trying to sell you anything. What's the key to your prison, Andy?" Moe Dee's voice stroked him.

A loon called to its mate across the lake; loons mated for life. Clear water lapped at the rocks.

Andy said, "Legs."

"And what do you want to be waiting for you when you break out?"

He took a deep breath and closed his eyes. For the first time in his life, he dared to give it voice, and the name felt like oil on his lips. "Jackie."

"Where you been? You okay?" Christine's voice trembled, but she smiled hopefully.

"Yeah, sorry. Went for a walk. And sorry about the, uh, outburst."

"It's okay."

He lowered himself beside her. "Where'd the other two go?"

"Oh, you know. Off that way."

Andy nodded, and his gut clenched. He said brightly, "Well, I hope they're not having sex. You know what happens to people who have sex in the woods."

"What?"

"They're the ones the slasher kills first."

Her eyes widened. "Really?"

"Yup, happens in all the movies."

She giggled. "Oh. I hate horror movies. Too scary. And, um ... Sorry I asked about that stuff. I was just curious, you know? Sensitive topic."

"It's okay."

She twirled her hair and relaxed.

They talked for a while. She was going to teach elementary school when she graduated. She loved Prince and Michael Jackson and she thought *Twilight* was the greatest novel ever written. She loved puppies and Chinese food and line dancing and loved her mother but hated her father because he drank too much and her brother never got any respect because he was gay, and Andy just let her talk.

After a while, he turned to her and discovered she was sitting very close, the diminishing fire reflected in her eyes. She took a deep breath, and the next thing he knew, her lips were on his. He tasted her mouth, pulled away for only a moment, then let it happen. He hadn't kissed a girl since prom when Pamela gave him a wine-soaked pity-French.

Hot, wet tongues slid back and forth, probing, hands reached, grasping, sliding, squeezing. Her breasts pressed against his chest, warm and soft and real, and their bodies gravitated closer. Their teeth touched, and their tongues wrestled clumsily, but for a while the world went away.

Voices echoed through the trees. "Oh, God, baby! Yes! Yes!"

"Ah, fuck! Oh, yeah!"

"Oh, my God!"

"Yeah! Yeah!"

And then the voices collapsed into gasping laughter and faded back into the whisper of the night.

Andy snapped away from her, wiped his mouth, rolled onto his knees, and used the log to push himself upright. His fists and teeth clenched.

Christine giggled. "Sounded like fun." She stood up. "Don't go far. I'm going to run to the little girl's room."

Andy took a deep breath and let her hurry off toward the outhouse about a hundred yards up the path.

He stood alone and reached into his pocket to feel the four little capsules, turning them over and over in his fingers.

The capsules dissolved quickly, tastelessly, in four glasses of beer. After Andy initiated a new but short-lived drinking game, all four of them drank just enough. The effects began within minutes. His crotch started to throb with heat and sparkly motes filled the air. He reached for one and it felt warm on his finger. Christine swayed to silent music, her head back.

"Wow!" Joe said. "Baby, I'm rock hard again! Check it

out!"

Jackie's eyes turned toward his crotch and glimmered. She reached for him.

Andy took her hand instead, and she turned toward him dreamily. He said, "Come on, you guys."

Christine's hand slid into his other. "Where we going?"

"I met this guy. He's having a little party and invited us. Come on, Joe."

"Party! All right! Help me up, baby. I'm all tingly."

Jackie took him by the hand and hauled him upright.

"Woo!" Joe wiggled his fingers before his eyes. "What the hell? Vapor trails *and* a woody!"

Jackie squeezed one of her breasts, eyes glazed. Christine giggled and purred, sliding against Andy, up and down.

"Come on." Andy tugged them toward the path, and they followed him.

By the time they reached the circle of fires glowing around Moe Dee's campsite, Andy's vision had grown foggy. That was a lot of fires for one guy. How many? Five? Sparks flickered at the periphery of his sight, embers rising skyward. His skin tingled with heat, and his erection throbbed against his zipper.

Moe Dee met them wearing only beach shorts, welcomed each of them with a warm embrace. His rippling body gleamed in the firelight. Andy had never hugged a man before, besides his dad. Moe Dee smelled like spices and expensive cologne. The flesh of his back was smooth and soft under Andy's hands, but covered a layer of muscle harder than anything he had ever felt. Like wood swathed in thin foam, not unlike Andy's first prosthetic legs. The women's hands lingered on Moe Dee's chest, on his shoulders, stroked his belly. He laughed, and his teeth gleamed, his eyes obsidian chips backlit with embers.

Andy's vision swirled and fogged, cleared and darkened in tantalizing cycles, and things began to happen quickly. A shirt came off. Jackie's naked breasts gleamed, perfect, Christine's smooshed across his back, naked, warm, rubbing. His hands were full of soft flesh.

Joe laughed. "Oh, baby, you look good!"

Andy rubbed his eyes. A woman's mouth was on him, Jackie's, licking, sucking. His jeans were open. Off.

He lay back on the leaf-shrouded earth, surrounded by fires.

Moe Dee laughed.

Jackie gasped.

Joe groaned.

Moans coalesced with clutching fingers.

Jackie's exquisite scent filled his nose. He buried his face in her hair, in her breasts, exactly as he had imagined they would be, clutched her to him. His heart thundered and his vision dimmed and throbbed.

His legs came off.

He lay on the ground, his stumps naked with the rest of him, and Jackie mounted him. His body seethed, every nerve-ending on fire. He thrust up against her, blindly, desperately, willing this all not to be a dream, not to be the cruelest acid trip of all time.

A strange moment of fleshy resistance met his penetration, but his hips thrust through it, driving up into her, and she gasped and cried out. Pulsing red light shot through him like a thousand exploding suns, and he cried out with her. Her voice sounded far away as if through a long culvert, and warm wetness slicked his hair and legs and scrotum.

Moe Dee breathed hot in his ear, smelling of cinnamon and cloves. "I can free you from your prison, Andy. Just say 'yes, do it.'"

"Yes! Do it!"

"Do you accept the cost?"

"Yes, anything!"

"Say, 'I accept.'"

"I accept!"

"Excellent."

Jackie gasped and moaned in his other ear, straining, shuddering, gasping little noises in the back of her throat. It was the most beautiful thing he had ever heard.

"Ah!" Joe's voice was distant but somewhere nearby. He coughed.

Christine giggled from over there. Or was it Jackie's voice. "Wow! Trippy!"

Jackie's face, mouth wide, glowing with ecstasy, hovering above his, rhythmic, driving down against him, the culmination of every dream he had ever had, ever would have.

Then like a bomb that goes off in its maker's hand, his orgasm ripped through him, blew him into a million bits of quivering sensation. His body bucked and nearly threw her off. She felt heavier on top of him than she should have, squishier. Light blazed. His back arched, his shoulders and the ends of his stumps pressing down against the earth. Lines of glowing red stretched from fire to fire beneath the carpet of leaves, around the circle, crossing under him. But he didn't care. Jackie was on top of him and he was still hard.

Something snapped at the ends of his legs and sensation exploded up his femurs. Spasms of agony or ecstasy.

The fires flared a deep red, but it must have been the 'H.' His heart pounded in his ears.

Jackie moaned and squeezed him into her, around him. He rolled on top of her.

The night deepened and Moe Dee's presence loomed nearby, taller than any man. Pale, blue-veined legs tipped in black hooves. The scents of coppery blood and musky sex thickened the air and Andy's erection.

Lightning slashed the sky and thunder echoed across the surface of the lake like the peals of an artillery barrage.

He took her again, this time from behind, and felt the warm, grainy softness of the moldy leaves under the soles of his feet.

Andy awoke to dim gray-blue sky, the scent of leaf mold in his nostrils. He lay on a dewy carpet of leaves, naked.

His feet were cold.

He rolled over onto his hands and knees, expecting a hangover from Hell, but felt no pain. Two pale shapes lay naked with him, surrounded by five gray piles of smoldering ash. Christine lay close beside him. Her groggy hand dimly reached for him, then returned to quiescence. Jackie's smooth back and naked buttocks lay near where Moe Dee's tent had stood. The tent was gone now.

Feet.

Knees.

"Oh. My. God."

He could hardly believe it.

His *feet* were cold!

He caught the whoop of elation in his throat and throttled it back to choked laughter.

He stood and touched his new legs, strong and firm. He jumped, he squatted, he tap-danced, giggling like a child. He breathed the forest air, and felt like a whole man for the first time in his life.

Wow, what a party.

He took a step toward Jackie, with the idea of kissing her awake, making love to her again. He could walk with her now, dance with her. But how in the hell was he going to explain what had happened below his knees? It was a miracle.

He'd have to think about it for a while, come up with some story, maybe go away for a couple of months to a "special clinic" or something, but in the meantime, he'd cover them up, pretend everything was normal, and go take a bath in the lake. His crotch was crusted with dried blood and fluids. What a party. He wondered vaguely where Joe was, but he picked up his jeans, shoes, and former legs, and headed back to their campsite.

No, he skipped. Like a six-year-old.

He stowed the prosthetics under the rear seat of the pickup and put his jeans, socks, and shoes on. The socks felt warm and soft, absolutely amazing. His shoes were too small, uncomfortable, pinching his toes, but he didn't dare let anyone see his feet until he figured out how to explain this.

The lake water was cold, clear, and he let new heights of invigoration wash through him. The sun came up as he floated dreamily on his back.

Jackie called down to him from the campsite. "Hey, Andy!"

"Good morning!"

"You seen Joe?"

"Not yet."

The two women's voices filtered through the trees to the water, quiet. From their tone, he didn't need to hear their words to know they were asking each other what the hell happened last night.

Christine called to him, "Come on, baby! We're making breakfast! Bacon and eggs!"

He felt like he could eat a horse, and then go for a five-mile run.

When he made his way back up to the campsite, Christine was nowhere to be seen, and Jackie had her cell phone in her hand. "I can't reach Joe!"

"I'm sure he's fine." He put his arm around her and rubbed her shoulder.

"But he's been gone over an hour, and he didn't take the truck."

"Probably passed out somewhere. He's a big boy. I'm sure he'll be awake soon enough."

She gave him a sheepish smile. "You've got an awfully big grin this morning."

"What a night, huh?"

"Yeah, holy shit. That was absolutely trippy. And where did that Moe Dee guy go anyway? He packed up and left while we were passed out?"

"I guess."

"Rude at best, really creepy at worst."

"I suppose so. But it was still an amazing night." He leaned forward to kiss her. She looked away and his lips fell on her cheek. A bolt of tension shot through him.

Christine came down the path, throwing her arms wide. "Morning, stud!" She embraced him and stuck her tongue in his ear, purring, nuzzling his hair.

An hour passed with no Joe. The sun rose higher, but it was still only eight a.m., early rising after a bender like that. Jackie started to pace, calling his phone until she heard it ringing from its place on the pickup dashboard.

Finally, Andy said, "Okay, I'll go look for him. He can't be far."

"We'll come, too," she said.

They searched the woods around their campsite, then searched Moe Dee's campsite, spiraling outward and outward, calling Joe's name. Another hour passed. Andy kept expecting him to march naked out of the woods, give them a salute and a crooked grin and announce that he was off to take a morning shit. It was still too early in the day to get worried. He'd known Joe to sleep off a drunk until two in the afternoon.

Jackie's worry seeped into Andy, dampening his enjoyment of how his legs managed the treacherous forest floor so easily. For the first time, he felt whole.

Jackie kept saying, "When we find him, I'm going to fucking kill him!"

Christine did her best to calm Jackie.

They searched up and down the shore of the lake, thinking maybe he had wandered off and fallen in the water.

By eleven o'clock, Andy had to admit he was getting worried too. Jackie called the county sheriff's office and then the state police, but, of course, they told her there was nothing they could do until Joe was missing for twenty-four hours.

Andy headed off toward the toilet to empty his bladder and gather his thoughts. What the hell would he do if something had happened to Joe? They were inextricable parts of each other's lives. He hoped that Joe wouldn't be sore about what happened last night. That had been some kind of full-fledged orgy. He didn't remember having sex with Christine, but she certainly acted as if they had. Everything was so fuzzy, he supposed it was possible. For Christ's sake, he woke up with legs! Anything was possible.

He stepped out of the stench-ridden outhouse and stopped as a medium-sized canine shape, gray and tan and lean, slunk out of the nearby bushes. A coyote. It paused, and its eyes glittered at him. His heart flipped over. A long strip of bloody flesh dangled from its jaws. It smiled, then took off running down the path away from him.

For almost a minute, Andy's lungs couldn't draw breath, and he stood frozen in place. His shoulders turned to cold lead. Finally, remembering the point at which the coyote had emerged, he thrust himself through the undergrowth and started to search.

J oe's face was barely recognizable, glazed eyes rolled back and staring upward, his face littered with leaves and detritus. Andy's gaze slid over the naked body, driven by a mind unable to fathom the wounds that had been wreaked. Until his gaze reached Joe's legs. Both legs ended at the knee, white stumps of blood-smeared femur, the surrounding flesh neatly sliced and covered with flies.

He reeled to the side and spewed bacon and eggs, heaving until his belly was empty, then heaving some more until he fell onto his side, gasping, tendrils of vomit falling across his cheek. Syllables without meaning dribbled from his mouth. Ten years of friendship tore through his mind, incidents and experiences, good times, family and friends. Tears streamed across his face. He pulled his new knees to his chest, tight against his stomach, and hugged them.

He ignored the footsteps approaching through the undergrowth. A spot of sunlight filtered through the canopy and fell warm across his cheek. A tear trickled through the spot.

"Andy? Is that you? Are you there? I thought I heard you yelling..."

The footsteps stopped a few paces away. Jackie screamed.

"Y ou're going to have to move, Andy," Moe Dee's voice said. "They're coming back."

Andy wanted to drown in the waste of the forest floor.

"What? No word of thanks?"

"Fuck you."

"Indeed. That is what I'm about, after all."

"Who are you?"

Moe Dee's shape loomed nearer. "I could tell you who I am, but I think you already know. Or at least, you're in the ball park."

Andy looked at him squarely. He was the most beautiful man Andy had ever seen, dressed in a white linen shirt, beach shorts, and black flip-flops, tall and hale and tanned. "You own my soul now?"

Moe Dee shrugged. "The trade in souls is a step above my rank. I merely set the hook and let you humans squirm yourselves to perdition. It so often takes only a nudge to send you spinning in the most interesting directions. Anything else I can do for you before I'm on my way?"

"Fuck you."

"Most impolite, Andy. I gave you everything you wanted."

"Take it back!" Spittle and vomit flew from his lips.

"Apologies, but it doesn't work that way. You are free now, just as you asked."

"Take them back! Bring Joe back!"

"Um, yes ... Joe. Unfortunate that he didn't survive my ministrations. He had so much life in him. Resurrection, however, is for the other team. They are yours now. Do with them as you will."

"Please." Andy was weeping.

Moe Dee started to turn away. "I suppose I must thank you for a wonderful evening. I did enjoy myself. It wouldn't have been possible without the energy of two virgins. And the energy of virgins is so ... intoxicating. And that Jackie, I can certainly see why you love her. She was quite a tidbit, didn't even mind when I cut off her lover's legs in front of her."

"Please take it back."

Moe Dee sighed. "I'm feeling generous, as you're my friend, and we've shared so much."

A choked gasp erupted from the body lying nearby. Joe screamed and heaved.

Moe Dee held out his hand, and black mist appeared around it, coalesced into a knife made of black steel that looked as ancient as Babylon, as long as his forearm. The glinting blade curved downward.

Spittle and dead leaves blew from Joe's face. "Oh, God! Oh, God! It hurts!" Fresh blood trickled from the gashes and symbols carved across his body.

Moe Dee tossed the knife near Andy, and its weight drove the point six inches into the soft earth. The hilt was black wood, carven with strange symbols. "I'll want that back when you're done." Then he walked off through the trees.

Andy took up the dagger.

Joe's eyes stared sightlessly at the underside of the forest canopy. There was no intellect in them. His chest heaved and gasped.

When Jackie and Christine found Andy again, he had sliced the legs of his jeans open to above the knee and had fashioned the denim into twin tourniquets. Blood trickled from one deep slice across the top of his kneecap.

Joe had lapsed into unconsciousness. His wounds had stopped bleeding. His breathing was ragged but steady.

Christine screamed and reeled to the side. "Oh, my God!

I'm gonna be sick!"

"I can't do it, Jackie." He sobbed once. "Please." He offered her the knife.

Her gaze went from the knife, to Joe's ravaged body, to Andy's feet. Recognition dawned in her eyes for only a moment before they turned cold and empty.

Author, freelance writer, award-winning screenwriter, poker player, biker, roustabout, and graduate of the Odyssey Writing Workshop, Travis Heermann is the author of numerous short stories appearing in such places as *Weird Tales*, Cemetery Dance's *Shivers Vol. VII*, and *Historical Lovecraft*, among others. He is the author of the The Ronin Trilogy, *Rogues of the Black Fury, The Wild Boys,* and *Snakes*. Aside from his fiction work, he has contributed to almost thirty roleplaying supplements from Alderac Entertainment, including their Legend of the Five Rings and d20 System game lines, plus the game content for White Wolf/CCP's EVE Online.

Find the author online!
Email: travis@travisheermann.com
Web: http://www.travisheermann.com
Blog: http://www.travisheermann.com/blog
Twitter: @TravisHeermann
Facebook: https://www.facebook.com/travis.heermann

OTHER TITLES BY TRAVIS HEERMANN
Available NOW from Damnation Books

"A fast-paced novel about love, loss, and the unforgettable scent of once being human, *The Wild Boys* is impossible to put down." - Shelly Li, Scholastic Award-winning author of *The Royal Hunter: Throne Under Siege*

"I recommend *The Wild Boys* for people who like thrillers, people who like horror, and people who want to read wild chase scenes with plucky heroines (and a dog)." - Kater Cheek, author of the Kit Melbourne series

"*Snakes* provokes a gut-wrenching emotional response, perhaps because by using snakes as a motif, it speaks to one of our most primitive fears. ... For a 30-page story to have such a deep, powerful and abiding effect shows that Travis Heermann is a master, ranking up there with Aesop and the Greek myth writers."- Rose Cimarron, Goodreads Reviewer

Available NOW from E-Reads

"Bold, colorful characters pull the reader into an unforgettable adventure with the perfect mix of suspense, intrigue, and action." - Jeanne Cavelos, author of *The Passing of the Techno-mages*

"Rogues of the Black Fury mixes a berserk action thriller sharp as a mercenary's sword with hard-bitten fantasy so gritty it might scour your bones clean by the time you're done." - Matt Forbeck, author of *The Amortals* and *Carpathia*

"Heermann's Rogues is epic, exciting, and a hell of a lot of fun! From the very beginning, the world he crafts feels alive and real. By the last page, I didn't want to leave. Adventure at its finest, honed to a gleaming bloody edge." - Marcus Pelegrimas, author of the Skinners series

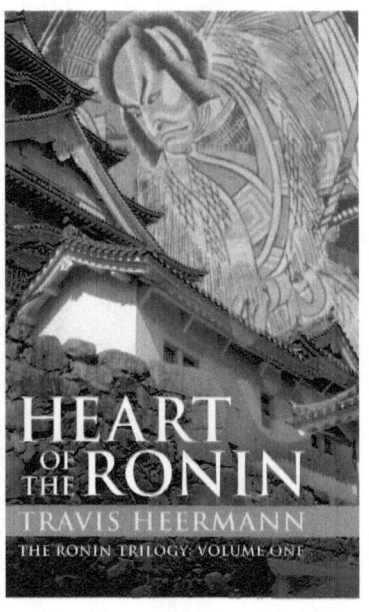

"A fusion of historical fiction and adventure fantasy, the first volume of Heermann's Ronin Trilogy is a page-turning folkloric narrative of epic proportions." - Publishers Weekly

"Full of sword battles, intrigue, romance and fantastic elements blending well with historical ones, *Heart of the Ronin* is a very impressive opening in the Ronin Trilogy. It's also a page turner that you can't put down and will leave readers begging for more."- Fantasy Book Critic

"*Heart of the Ronin* is a solid, likeable adventure story, sure to please fans of Japanese culture and fantasy readers alike." - Adventures in Sci-Fi Publishing

www.ingramcontent.com/pod-product-compliance
Lightning Source LLC
Chambersburg PA
CBHW020611130626
46552CB00007B/3148